VISIT THE EIGHTH WONDER OF THE WORLD: THE WONDERLAND ODDITY MUSEUM

SEE! Shrunken heads from the wilds of Borneo

SEE! The Declaration of Independence written on a penny

SEE! A two-headed mouse pickled in a jar

SEE! The crown once worn by the Queen of Octavia

SEE! The Thing. What is it? Where did it come from?

Plus thousands of other oddities collected from the four corners of the world!

Open Daily 10–5 at Smuggler's Cove

THE THING UPSTAIRS

STEPHEN MOOSER

Rainbow Bridge®
Troll Associates

LIBRARY OF CONGRESS CATALOGING-IN-PUBLICATION DATA
Mooser, Stephen.
  The thing upstairs / Stephen Mooser.
     p.   cm.
  Summary: Aspiring writer Wesley Shakespeare has a vivid
imagination, but when he agrees to write and perform in a play to
raise money for the restoration of the Wonderland Oddity Museum,
even he gets some surprises.
  ISBN 0-8167-3421-6 (pbk.)
  [1. Plays—Fiction.   2. Authorship—Fiction.   3. Mystery and
detective stories.]   I. Title.
PZ7.M78817Tk   1994
[Fic]—dc20   93-50676

Copyright © 1994 by Stephen Mooser.
Cover illustration copyright © 1994 by Tim Jacobus.

Published by Troll Associates, Inc. Rainbow Bridge is a
trademark of Troll Associates.

Printed in the United States of America.

10 9 8 7 6 5 4 3 2 1

For Sue Shields and
her students at
Fairview Elementary,
Anchorage, Alaska.

Table of Contents

Chapter One
SHAKESPEARE

Whew! It was so hot even my goldfish was sweating. Crimson Beach had had three days of hundred-degree temperatures and the weatherman was predicting at least three more. My room felt ready to burst into flames, but I didn't dare leave. Not till I'd finished writing the latest Wesley Shakespeare adventure. I'd been plunked down at my desk all morning in nothing but a T-shirt and underwear, struggling to finish my story. Luckily, I was almost to the end.

Through the open window I could see my neighbors, Nick and Sarah, seated in the shade of a giant oak. Sarah was propped up against the tree cooling herself with an old paper fan, and Nick was busy chewing on a fat blade of grass. As always, he was clutching his stuffed white puppy, Killer, in his arms. The two of them were never apart.

I turned away from the window and gave myself a wink in the big mirror above my desk. My long face was beaded with sweat, and my wild red hair looked like windblown flames. William Shakespeare stared out from my T-shirt above the words "The World's Greatest Writer." Someday I was going to be a great writer, too. Someday soon.

The end! I wrote down the words in my notebook.

"Perfect," I said, quickly reading the completed work. "Another great piece of writing, if I say so myself."

I couldn't wait to share my masterpiece with the world. Hurriedly I pulled on a pair of too big pants, hurtled down the stairs, and dashed out of the house.

"Nick! Sarah!" I screamed, running wildly across the lawn as if the house behind me was about to blow. "You're in luck! It's time for the latest Wesley Shakespeare adventure!"

Nick squinted at me through his big round glasses as I skidded to a stop in front of them, one hand clutching my notebook, the other gripping my beltless pants. Sarah just kept on fanning. She was wearing shorts, a green army T-shirt, and a spotted camouflage cap. Her ponytail dangled out the back. There was a big scar on her chin from a dog bite two years earlier. Like me, Sarah was in the sixth grade. Unlike me, she wasn't very excited about my writing.

I paused to catch my breath. "Ready to hear the new story?"

"No," muttered Sarah. "Listen, Wesley, just because you have the last name of a famous writer, that doesn't mean you are one."

"But this is my best one yet," I said, pleading my case. "I promise, you'll love it."

"What's it about?" asked Nick. He had a round face, huge ears, and a flattop. In the fall he'd be starting third grade.

"Picture this," I said, holding out my hand toward some invisible scene. "Two little puppies, alone in a little boat, far out at sea. Want to hear more?"

"Of course. Go on," said Nick, clutching his own stuffed puppy to his chest.

Good old Nick. I could always count on him. He was a sucker for dog stories.

"What happened next?" he asked.

I grinned and flipped open the notebook with one hand, keeping the other one on my pants.

Then I cleared my throat and began. "After two weeks at sea, the puppies suddenly found themselves in the middle of a horrible hurricane. Waves taller than the Empire State Building crashed all around them. Killer winds tossed their boat around like a toothpick. Raindrops big as water balloons smashed onto their furry little heads."

Nick's eyes were round as wagon wheels behind his glasses. "Wha . . . wha . . . what happened next?" he asked.

"You know what happens next," said Sarah. "Wesley's stories always turn out the same."

"Not this time," I said. "Listen up. The story is about to get super scary."

Nick shivered. He hugged his stuffed puppy. He didn't like scary things.

I pressed my face right into the notebook and went on excitedly. "Suddenly, out of nowhere, came a lightning bolt! *Kee-rack!* It split the little boat in two."

Nick gasped. Sarah yawned.

"Thunder and lightning were everywhere!" I shouted.

"*KA-BOOM!*" I yelled, clapping my hands for a sound effect.

12

Whoops! To clap my hands I'd had to let go of my pants. Down they came, like a dropped curtain.

Sarah laughed. Nick laughed, too.

"Yikes!" I said, staring down at my blue, polka-dotted underwear. I felt my face go red.

Nick and Sarah couldn't stop giggling.

I quickly hitched up my pants. Then I cleared my throat and continued on as if a second earlier I hadn't been half naked.

"Suddenly a huge wave came crashing over the burning boat and threw the puppies into the sea! The poor little things yelped and barked, but no one heard them."

"Wha . . . what happened next to the poor little dogs?" asked Nick, nearly squeezing his stuffed puppy in two.

I closed my notebook and recited the rest by heart. "There they were paddling around in the cold stormy sea," I said, staring off, watching the drama unfold in my mind. "The waves grew bigger. The wind howled louder. The rain rained harder. The end!" I smiled, then bowed low and awaited the applause.

None came.

"Well," I said, at last. "Did you like the story?"

"Your story was no fair," said Nick angrily. He waved his dog in my face. "Stories have to have endings."

"Wait a minute," I said, confused. "Isn't 'The end!' an ending?"

"Not when it comes in the middle of the story," said Sarah.

"Great stories deserve great endings," said Nick. "And surprise endings are the best of all."

"Your stories always turn out the same," said Sarah. "Do us a favor. Just once, put a real ending on one of your stories. Go ahead, surprise us."

"That reminds me! I've got a giant surprise!" I said, clapping my hands.

Whoops! Down came my pants again, like a flag down a pole. Sarah rolled her big brown eyes. "I hope your underpants aren't the surprise."

I groaned, bent over, and awkwardly yanked up my pants.

"Guess what?" I said, my hand firmly gripping my waistband. "My family just inherited Wonderland, the amusement park. I'm going there tomorrow."

"An amusement park!" said Nick. "Cool!"

I crossed my heart. "I swear. It's true. It belonged to my great-uncle Max before he died."

"Is it in Florida?" asked Nick.

"It's right here, in Crimson Beach," I said. I pointed down the road. "My father says it's at Smuggler's Cove."

"I didn't know there was an amusement park there," said Sarah.

"Well, there is, and now my family owns it," I said.

Nick whistled. "Could you get us free rides?"

"Are you kidding? All my buddies ride for free," I said, playing the big shot.

Nick shivered. "The rides won't be too scary, will they?"

"I bet some of them are super scary," I said. "Of course, to be honest, I've never been out there."

"Just to be safe, I think that Killer and I will just ride on the merry-go-round," said Nick, gazing down at his stuffed puppy.

"Ride it all you want," I said. I slapped my chest. "Tomorrow all the wonders of Wonderland are on me." I looked at Sarah, then at Nick. "So will you come out there with me? Is it a deal?"

"I don't know," said Sarah. She tilted back her spotted green cap and studied me long and hard. "Are you sure this isn't just another one of your stupid stories?"

"No way. This is the real thing," I said. "What do you have to lose? Everything is going to be free."

"Well," said Sarah, "I guess there isn't any harm in checking it out."

"Of course there isn't," I said. "Believe me, Wonderland will be an unforgettable experience for all of us."

Chapter Two

THUNDER

A clap of thunder, loud as a dynamite blast, awakened me at dawn. During the night a summer storm had swept over Crimson Beach, bringing with it a symphony of thunder and a welcome relief from the heat.

I dressed quickly, pulling on my Shakespeare T-shirt and a pair of long, checked shorts. Then I grabbed a bagel and banana breakfast and hurried across the street.

"Sarah! Nick! Let's go!" I shouted, standing on their lawn.

A few minutes later Sarah appeared at an upstairs window in her pajamas.

"We have to leave now," I said. "A storm's coming."

Sarah rubbed the sleep from her eyes and glanced up at the clouds.

"For heaven's sake, Wesley, it's six-thirty in the morning," she said. "Wonderland probably isn't even open yet."

"They'll open it for me," I said. "Get Nick. Let's go."

Sarah growled and disappeared back inside. Fifteen minutes later the three of us were on our bikes heading down Rose Avenue toward Smuggler's Cove.

"How come you've never been out to your great-uncle's place?" Nick shouted, pulling up alongside me. Killer was strapped onto his bike rack.

"My parents never mentioned the amusement park. Dad didn't like Uncle Max or his business," I replied, admiring my reflection in Nick's big round glasses. I had a writer's face, I thought: a long nose for sniffing out a story, deep eyes so I could see through to the truth, and big ears for picking up juicy bits of dialogue.

"How can someone not like an amusement park?" asked Nick, as we swung our bikes around a corner and onto Ocean Drive.

"My dad hates show business," I said. "He thinks entertainment is a gigantic waste of time."

"Really?" said Nick. "Does that mean he never goes to movies?"

"Never goes to anything," I said. "And he doesn't like us to go either. I think we're the only people in town who don't own a TV."

"Nothing on the tube but nonsense," my dad once said. "We won't have any idiot boxes in this house, no way!"

I guess it wasn't so bad, though. Without a TV around, I got to read a lot, and books are what inspired me to become a writer. I'd been writing things for as long as I could remember. Mom was real encouraging and so was my little sister, Beth. But Dad was another story.

I don't think a day went by that he didn't try to get me to quit writing.

"A waste of time," he'd say. "Besides, you can't make any money at it."

Dad worked at the bank in town. All he ever thought about was money. I'm not sure I ever heard him laugh. Not once.

Just as we were passing the Ocean Drive Dairy Bar a flash of lightning dead ahead nearly blinded me.

"Uh-oh. That looked as if it hit around

Smuggler's Cove," said Nick. He shivered. "Maybe we ought to turn back."

"Nick's right!" shouted Sarah, from somewhere behind me. "It's going to pour. We could be stuck out there all day."

"So what?" I said. "If it rains we'll just stay inside the video arcade."

"What? There's a video arcade?" said Nick.

"There must be," I said.

"Can we play for free?" asked Nick.

"All day long," I said. "Remember, me and my parents own the place."

I chuckled to myself. Maybe Dad didn't have a sense of humor, but Uncle Max must have. Why else would he have left a place like Wonderland to my father? Why else would he have stuck such an entertainment hater with the biggest center of fun and games in Crimson Beach?

The thought of free video games spurred us on. We bore down on the pedals and raced the rest of the way to Smuggler's Cove.

As we soon discovered, however, there was no need to hurry. Smuggler's Cove turned out to be as deserted as a ghost town. When we pulled into the little dirt parking lot, only the sea gulls, the sand, and the waves were there to greet us.

Sarah sat astride her bike, her ponytail flapping in the wind, giving me a look of exasperation. "Well, at least we won't have to stand in line for the free rides," she said sarcastically.

"I don't see any video arcade," said Nick. He wrinkled his face and squinted through his glasses. "I don't even see any buildings."

I clucked my tongue and rolled my eyes. Sometimes my friends were such dolts. "Wonderland isn't on the beach," I explained. I pointed across the way into a tangled forest of pine and brush. "It's back there, in the woods."

"Yeah, sure," said Sarah. "Give us a break, Wesley. Why aren't there any signs?"

A roll of thunder shook the ground. The clouds looked ready to burst.

"Did you make this whole thing up?" asked Sarah. She narrowed her eyes. "I hope this isn't another one of your stories without an ending."

"No. I swear," I said. I crossed my heart with one of my long, spidery fingers. "My dad said it was here. He wouldn't lie."

I dropped my bike and walked to the edge of

the woods. At first I didn't see anything. Fortunately, Nick wasn't nearly so blind.

"Look!" he exclaimed, pointing with his stuffed dog. "There it is!"

I squinted and followed his outstretched hand. Sure enough, about thirty feet into the woods was an old, two-story wooden building hunched down among the brush and the weeds. Two big windows on the second floor, empty of glass, stared out at us with a mournful gaze.

"This must be the haunted house part of the amusement park," I said, locating a thin trail into the brush. "Follow me. This will be fun."

Nick gulped and held his ground.

"I'm not going near any haunted house," he said. "Call me when you find the video arcade."

"Can't you see? There is no video arcade," said Sarah. "There's no Wonderland either. That house may be haunted, but it's not part of any amusement park."

Nick looked down at his little stuffed puppy and moaned.

"Sometimes I wish I had a real dog," he said. "A real dog could protect me from trouble."

Sarah sighed. She knew how much Nick wanted a pet. We all did. But ever since she'd been bitten on the chin that day, her parents had forbidden dogs in the house. I think Nick kind of resented Sarah for that, even though it really wasn't her fault. Naturally, Sarah felt bad about it too, though there was nothing she could do about it.

"Come on," said Sarah, putting her arm around Nick's shoulder. "I'll protect you."

Nick looked up into his sister's face. "Thanks," he said.

It took us a few minutes to pick our way through the brush and the rocks to the old building. Up close, the place looked as if it had been abandoned for decades. The outside was covered with splintered boards, some of them sprinkled with flakes of old, brown paint. Every window had been broken, and the front door was hanging cockeyed by a single hinge. Above the doorway, in yellow letters so faint they could barely be read, were the words WONDER-LAND ODDITY MUSEUM.

"I guess maybe I don't own an amusement park after all," I said. "I own an oddity museum."

Nick crept up to the doorway and peered into the darkened interior of the building. "What's an oddity museum?" he asked.

I shrugged. "I'm not sure, but it's my guess we won't find any video games in there."

"Or any rides, either," said Sarah. "The only things you might find in an old place like this are ghosts."

Nick shivered. "Let's get out of here," he said.

I poked my head into the open doorway and glanced around. "There's nothing in here," I said. I turned and shrugged. "Sorry, guys. I guess we'll just have to go back home."

"Go home? After we came all this way?" said Sarah. "Don't you want to at least look around inside?"

"Not particularly," said Nick.

"What's there to see?" I asked.

"I can't believe you," said Sarah. She stepped inside. "You're ready to halt our adventure before we get to the exciting conclusion. This day needs an ending, just like a good story."

She waved for us to follow. "Come on, men! Attack!"

Sarah was always playing the soldier. Her dad was in the army and someday she wanted to be in the military, too. She liked wearing army caps and T-shirts, but I think she liked giving orders even more.

Nick watched her disappear into the creepy old museum, then turned to me. "I'm not going in there. No way."

I swallowed and peered deep into the gloomy interior of the broken-down building. I wasn't so sure I wanted to go in either.

KA-BANG! A clap of thunder exploded above our heads like a bomb. An instant later the skies opened up and rain poured down as if someone had overturned a tub of water.

Nick and I leaped into the building as if we'd been poked. Like it or not, we'd just become guests at the Wonderland Oddity Museum.

Chapter Three

THE WONDERLAND ODDITY MUSEUM

Like a wet dog, I shook the rain from my hair and looked around the museum. At first glance it didn't appear as if anyone had been inside in years. Then a bolt of lightning lit one of the walls and I saw a slash of red graffiti. OUTLAWS RULE, it said. The paint looked fresh.

"Who are the Outlaws?" asked Nick.

"I don't know, but they don't sound very nice," said Sarah.

"Whoever they are, they've been trespassing on my property," I said. I made a fist. "If I catch them, *pow*! They better look out."

"I think we're the ones who should be looking out," said Nick. He pointed at the graffiti. "When they say 'Outlaws rule' I think they mean it."

KA-BOOM! Another bolt of lightning followed by a clap of thunder split the summer air, shaking the old building.

Nick whimpered and clutched Killer to his chest.

"I have a feeling we're going to be here for a while," said Sarah.

After my eyes finally adjusted to the dim light, I looked around and surveyed my property. From what I could tell, the whole first floor was one big room, nearly empty except for a rickety staircase against the back wall. The room itself was a mess. The floorboards were cracked and splintered and in some places weeds were growing up through the holes. A pile of bottles and rags littered one corner. The Outlaws' garbage dump, I figured.

"You know, I bet we could fix this up," I said, waving my arm around the room. "All we need is a rug, some paint, a few nails, maybe a light or two, and we could reopen this place." I turned to Sarah and rubbed my hands together. "What do you think? Wouldn't it be fun to run an Oddity Museum?"

"I think you're forgetting something," said Sarah.

"We'll paint it bright red and put a big neon sign on top," I went on. I stared off into the distance, picturing the finished building bathed in a neon glow. "We'll call it Wesley's Oddity Museum!"

"But Wesley," said Sarah, "you're forgetting something."

I scratched at my red curls and turned. "What did I forget?"

"The end. The part you always forget. You may have a museum, but you don't have any oddities."

"Hmmmm," I said.

Nick pointed out the door with his thumb. "Can we go now? It's almost stopped raining."

The rain had slowed to a trickle, but I wasn't ready to leave. Not till I'd gone upstairs. I grabbed hold of the rickety railing and peered up the steps. "Let's see what's hiding on the second floor. Who knows? Maybe there's a treasure chest up there."

"Maybe there's a bat," said Nick. "Or an entire motorcycle gang called the Outlaws." He walked over and stared up the stairs. "What if they're waiting up there to rob us?"

"Rob us of what?" I said. "Besides, it's early.

Gang members like to sleep in. They're probably all home in bed somewhere."

I put a foot on the bottom step and tested it to make sure the rotten wood wouldn't collapse. It didn't.

"Let's take a look," I said. "If we're lucky maybe we'll find some oddities."

Sarah led us up the stairs. Crouched low, a pretend rifle in her hands, she cleared the way for me and Nick. I don't think Nick wanted to see the second floor, but he didn't want to stay downstairs all by himself either.

As it turned out, the second floor was a lot like the first: big, open, and filled with dirt and trash. Four big broken windows let in light. Against the back wall a large empty closet, its door standing open, was surrounded by more crude graffiti. OUTLAWS HAVE THE MOST BRINS, said one of the scrawls.

"What's a brin?" asked Nick.

"I think they meant brains," said Sarah. "But they don't have enough of them to spell."

"Hey! Look at this," I said, calling Nick and Sarah over to a torn, faded poster I'd just discovered tacked to the wall. "It's all about my uncle's Oddity Museum."

Sarah and Nick came over and together we read the poster:

VISIT THE EIGHTH WONDER OF THE WORLD:
THE WONDERLAND ODDITY MUSEUM
>   SEE!   Shrunken heads from the wilds of Borneo
>   SEE!   The Declaration of Independence written on a penny
>   SEE!   A two-headed mouse pickled in a jar
>   SEE!   The crown once worn by the Queen of Octavia
>   SEE!   The Thing. What is it? Where did it come from?
> Plus thousands of other oddities
> collected from the four corners of the world!
> Open Daily 10-5 at Smuggler's Cove

By the time I'd finished reading, my mouth had flopped open like an oven door. "That stuff sounds so neat. I'd give anything to see that two-headed mouse."

"I'd rather have the crown," said Sarah. She shut her eyes and pretended to crown herself the Queen of Octavia. "I'd live in a castle and everything."

Nick pressed his face to the poster. "Where is Octavia anyway? Is that a real country?"

"Sure it is," I said quickly. "My uncle wouldn't make up something like that."

Actually, I didn't know that for a fact. Dad never talked about Uncle Max. And I'd never met him.

Sarah poked her pretend rifle into the closet and looked around. "What do you think ever happened to all those shrunken heads?"

"Or to The Thing?" I said. "What do you suppose that was anyway?"

"Sounds to me like some kind of monster," said Sarah.

"That's my theory, too," I said. "What do you think, Nick?"

Nick swallowed and looked around. "You know what I think? I think we ought to scoot on out of here. This place isn't a museum, it's a house of horrors."

I looked out a smashed window and stared deep into the surrounding woods. The Oddity Museum was no house of horrors to me. As a writer I saw it as a place of pure inspiration.

"You know what? When I get home I'm going to write a book about The Thing." I turned back and raised my hand in an elegant flourish. "I predict it will be my greatest story ever. It'll have everything: action, adventure, humor, even love!"

"Make sure it also has an ending," said Sarah.

"Of course it will have an ending," I said. I put my hands on my hips and raised my chin. "Don't you think I know how to write a story?"

Sarah chuckled. "Sure, Wesley, whatever you say."

I sighed. Being a writer was tough, especially when no one believed in you.

Sarah kicked shut the closet door. "There's nothing more to see here," she said. "All right, soldiers, let's go."

"Good idea!" said Nick. He and Killer streaked down the stairs and out the front door in six giant steps. By the time Sarah and I got outside he was already halfway back to the bikes, blazing a trail through the woods as if a pack of wolves was nipping at his heels.

I listened to him crashing through the trees, then sniffed the sweet, heavy air, fresh with the scent of new rain and damp earth.

"Maybe Nick doesn't want to see that two-headed mouse or say hello to The Thing, but I sure would," I said. I shook my head. "My uncle really collected some weird things, didn't he?"

"Where do you suppose everything went?" asked Sarah, pausing in the clearing. "Stuff like that usually doesn't just up and disappear."

"Maybe Uncle Max gave everything to my dad," I said. I chuckled at the thought. "Maybe that two-headed mouse is sitting in the back of our refrigerator next to the pickles."

Sarah laughed. "Remind me never to eat at your house again."

We started back to Smuggler's Cove where Nick and our bikes were waiting. I turned back for a final look at the Wonderland Oddity Museum, and gasped!

Maybe my eyes were playing tricks, but I was almost certain I saw a dark, hairy face looking back at me from one of the second-story windows. I shook my head to make sure I wasn't dreaming. When I looked back again, the creature was gone.

"Maybe it's just my writer's wild imagination," I thought. But deep down I wondered if I'd just caught a glimpse of The Thing.

Chapter Four
INVISIBLE BUGS

On the way home we made a detour at Columbus Street and wheeled into the Burger World parking lot. It was getting hot again, and steamy, too. We just couldn't pass up Burger World's cold drinks and air conditioning.

I guess we weren't the only ones in Crimson Beach who wanted to cool off. The place was jammed. Only three clerks were working behind the counter and the lines were moving somewhere between the speed of a glacier and a lazy snail.

"I wonder if Uncle Max really did give my dad some of that stuff from the museum," I said as we inched along. "I'd sure like to know where it is, especially if we're going to reopen the place."

Nick looked back at me. His eyes seemed

even bigger than normal behind his thick glasses. "Do you think he really might have those shrunken heads?"

"I hope so," I said, raising my voice over the clamor in the restaurant. "If I could find them I'd string those shriveled-up noggins onto a rope and wear them like a necklace."

"That would be so cool," said Nick.

An old lady in front of us turned and gave us a quizzical look. A little boy in the next line made a face.

"But wouldn't a shrunken head necklace smell?" asked Nick in all sincerity.

"Oh, boy, would it," I said, raising my voice another octave. "That's why I'd have to keep it in the refrigerator when I wasn't wearing it. Otherwise those heads would just start rotting away."

Nick held Killer up to his face. "Eeee-yew!"

Everyone was looking now. Some people might have been getting sick. I was writing a story for a real audience!

"Think about it," I continued, enjoying the attention. "Your necklace would start disappearing before your eyes. One day all the eyes would fall out. The next day you'd lose the ears."

"And after that the noses!" said Nick. "Cool!"

The lady in front of us turned, gave us a look of horror, then scurried away, tightly clutching her purse.

We moved up a space.

I laughed, then put a finger down my throat and pretended to throw up. "Gross! Could you picture me in front of the class giving a report with a string of rotting heads around my neck?"

"Cool!" said Nick.

"Dinosaurs lived millions of years ago," I said, giving my pretend report in a deep voice. "Whoops! There goes an ear off my necklace." I laughed.

"Yuck!" said Sarah. "That's enough. I'm losing my appetite."

"Yeah, watch your language," said a short, squat man with a thin mustache at the front of the next line. He was surrounded by six little kids, and every one of them was staring our way, open-mouthed. "My family came here to eat."

"So did I!" said a woman in a spotless white tennis outfit. "But now I'm not hungry!" She snorted, then turned around and stomped out of the restaurant.

"Gee, what got into them?" I asked as we moved up again.

Sarah rolled her eyes. "Maybe people don't enjoy hearing about shrunken heads while they're standing in a food line," she said.

"All right, all right," I said. "I won't talk about those heads anymore."

The crowd gave a collective sigh of relief.

"What I *am* going to talk about is that two-headed mouse," I said. I rubbed my chin. "How do you suppose they preserved him, in pickle juice?"

"Change that order! Hold the pickles," said the man in front of us to the clerk behind the counter. He turned around and glared. "And I used to love pickles, too."

"Gee, I'm sorry," I said. I looked around at the crowd for sympathy. "Did I say something wrong?"

"Yes," they all shouted in reply. About ten people, their faces pale, stepped out of line and walked out of Burger World, probably never to return.

For a second it looked like we were suddenly going to be moving straight to the counter.

Then, in a flash, two kids jumped into line ahead of us and began placing their orders with the clerk.

"Hey!" I said, recognizing them both. "No cutting!"

Sarah recognized them, too. "Teddy! Will! No fair. Go to the back of the line. That's an order. Move it!"

"Yeah," said Nick, in a whisper. He was scared of them both. Most of our friends were.

"Buzz off," said one of the kids, turning around. His name was Teddy LaBone and he was a year ahead of us in school. So was his friend, Will Pickens. Teddy was dressed in his usual uniform: a black derby hat, a pair of white gloves, and a sour expression. Will had a short haircut and a thin nose. He was always trying to look tough, but with his round rosy cheeks and sparkling eyes he had a hard time pulling it off.

"We've been standing here for fifteen minutes," I said. I reached out and poked Teddy on the back of the neck. "Wait your turn like everyone else."

Teddy wheeled around and glared. The clerk, a tall kid wearing a floppy hat in the shape of a hamburger, stood frozen, his mouth open, a finger raised, awaiting Teddy's food order.

"Don't you, ever, ever touch me again," said Teddy coldly, slowly massaging the back of his neck.

Nick gulped and took a step back, but I held my ground.

"He doesn't like to be touched," explained Will. "He doesn't like other people's germs."

Teddy's body shuddered. "I hate the thought of invisible bugs walking around on my skin. Everybody does."

"I don't. In fact, I sort of like germs, especially the slimy ones with wiggly bodies," I said.

Teddy shuddered.

I grinned. Teddy had made a career out of pushing people around, me included. Now I saw a way to push him back, using a writer's favorite weapon—words.

"I breed germs for pets," I said. "If I'd known you didn't like them, I wouldn't have given you so many just now."

Teddy winced and started wildly swatting the back of his neck as if it was crawling with slugs.

"Whew, you really are weird, aren't you?" I said.

"What did you say?" barked Teddy, dancing in place as he swatted away.

Before I could reply the clerk cut in. "I'm sorry, sir. But what would you like to eat?"

Teddy thought for a moment, then growled at the clerk and turned to go. "Come on, Will. Let's get out of this germ-infested dump."

"But I'm hungry," whined Will. "Why can't we—"

"I said, let's go," said Teddy. He jerked his gloved thumb toward the door. "Move! This punk just ruined my meal."

Will shrugged and followed, head lowered, like a sad little puppy.

We moved up to the front. The clerk behind the counter squinted at the empty restaurant and shook his head. "Hey, where did all the people go?"

"They got scared off," I said.

"Scared off?" said the clerk. He adjusted his hamburger hat and studied us for a moment with a pair of dark, sunken eyes. "What scared them?"

"Germs," I said.

"Shrunken heads," said Sarah.

"Pickled mice," said Nick.

"Oh," said the clerk. He drew in a deep breath, let it out slowly, then plastered his best Burger World smile on his face. "Well, then. What would you like to eat today?"

41

Chapter Five
THE NEW STORY

I couldn't get the Oddity Museum out of my head. Nor could I forget the hairy face I'd seen at the window. What had it been? A shadow? My imagination? The Thing?

It was driving me crazy. I had to find out what The Thing was supposed to be. If what I'd seen was really the ex-star of the museum, then I was sitting on a gold mine. If The Thing was a creature from outer space or even from prehistoric times, then he could easily be worth a million bucks. Maybe more!

I didn't believe I could count on Nick to help me capture such a scary beast, but I did think Sarah might be willing.

As it turned out, she didn't need much convincing. All I had to do was offer her a split of the profits.

"Half a million dollars is a lot of money," she said. "With that kind of dough, I could probably even find a dog for Nick, one that I wouldn't be scared of."

"What kind would that be?" I asked.

"A Mexican toothless," she said, laughing.

I invited Sarah over that evening so we could map out a strategy for capturing The Thing. What I didn't tell her was that another event was also scheduled for that evening: the reading of my latest story, "The Thing." I considered it my masterpiece.

After dinner that night my mom, my dad, and my little sister, Beth, gathered in the living room for the reading of my story. Dad, as usual, was dressed as if he were going to a funeral. Although he'd gotten off work at the bank hours earlier, he was still wearing a black suit coat that hung off his skinny frame like a scarecrow's oversized jacket.

He was closest to the door when Sarah knocked.

"Who's there?" he asked, opening it up a crack. "What do you want?"

"It's me," I heard Sarah say. "Sarah Hawkins, from across the street."

Dad opened the door wider and studied her carefully, making sure, I guess, that she wasn't a mass murderer disguised as a nice little neighbor girl.

"Did you come for the reading?" he asked, finally pulling the door the rest of the way open and inviting her in.

"What reading?" asked Sarah cautiously. She took off her camouflage hat, shook out her ponytail, and looked around the room. Eventually her eyes fell on me.

I waved my black notebook. "You're just in time," I said.

Sarah groaned.

"Wesley's about to read us a new story," said my father. He pointed to the couch where my mother and Beth were already seated. "Please, sit down."

Sarah paused on her way to the couch and slowly looked me up and down. I couldn't tell if she was just admiring the striped tie I'd put on over my Shakespeare T-shirt or silently berating me for tricking her into the reading. I do know this: She wasn't smiling.

Dad sat down in the big chair in the corner and folded his hands in his lap. "Wesley promises us that this time he's written a real story," he said.

"Wesley always writes real stories," said my mom. "Why would you say his stories aren't real?"

"Because they never have endings," said my father. "Real stories have beginnings, middles, and ends—especially ends."

"I like surprise endings best of all," said Sarah, taking her place on the couch alongside Beth.

"I like surprises, too," said Beth.

Sarah leaned over till she was nose to nose with Beth. "Boo!" she shouted.

Beth jumped a foot.

When she came down she put a hand to her heart. "Why'd you do that?"

"Because you said you liked surprises," said Sarah. She looked around and smiled. No one smiled back. Obviously, Sarah had forgotten that the Shakespeare family had been absent when senses of humor were passed out.

"Well," I said, loudly clearing my throat. "Shall we begin?"

"By all means, dear," said Mom, folding her hands neatly in her lap. "Let's hear the latest W. Shakespeare adventure."

I bowed to the audience and opened my notebook.

"The title of my new story is 'The Thing'!" I said, shouting out the title. I looked from face to face, then lowered my voice. "It was late one cold and stormy night in the Wonderland Oddity Museum. Not a creature was stirring. Not even a two-headed mouse."

"Is this a Christmas story?" asked Beth, raising her hand.

"Hardly," I said. I bent over, cackled, then wiggled my eyebrows. "It's a horror story."

Beth gulped and wrapped her arms around her knees.

"Suddenly, there came a knock at the door," I said, going on. "Then another. The knocks grew louder, and louder, and LOUDER!" I screamed. "Then all at once—*KA-BANG!*—the door splintered into a million pieces."

"What happened next?" asked my mother.

"Into the room came a horrible creature covered with furry warts," I said, making a face. I imagined my Adam's apple was bobbing up and down like an elevator with the hiccups. It did that a lot whenever I got excited. "The creature looked around and roared. Arrrrgh!"

47

Beth put her hands over her eyes.

My dad began nervously chewing on his thumb.

"'I am The Thing!' cried the awful beast," I said, my voice rising. "The end!"

Everyone leaned forward.

"Go on," said Mom, gesturing with her hands. "It's just starting to get good."

"What happened next?" asked Beth, peeking out from between her fingers. "I'll try not to be too scared. Go on. Tell us."

I slowly closed my book. "There's nothing more to tell," I said. "Didn't you hear what I said? The end!"

Everyone just stared.

"A story needs to have a real ending," said my father. "You can't stop something in the middle. When I work at the bank I count all the money. I don't stop in the middle. If I did I'd be fired."

I moaned and dropped my head. Why couldn't Dad say something nice about my writing, just once?

"I don't understand why you waste your time making up these silly stories," said my father, launching into his usual lecture. "The way to make money is with money. That's why I work at the bank."

"But I like to write," I said softly. I looked at Beth and got a smile in return. At least she supported me. At least she understood how I felt.

"Entertainment!" thundered my father, dismissing it with the back of his hand. "Hummpf! A waste of everyone's time."

"Maybe your next story could tell us a little more about The Thing," suggested Mom gently.

"What would there be to tell?" I said.

Mom shrugged. "I don't know. Where is The Thing from? What does he look like? What does he like to do?"

I shook my head. "I don't know any of that stuff," I said. I looked over at Dad. "Did you ever see The Thing at Uncle Max's museum? According to the poster, he was one of the stars."

Dad rolled his eyes. "As far as I knew, your Uncle Max invented half the stuff in that museum. To tell you the truth, I never set foot in that awful place. The two of us never got along. He was too much of a dreamer for me."

I ran my hand through my hair and sighed. I had the feeling that I was probably too much of a dreamer for him, too.

"Uncle Max was a smart man," said my father. "He just never knew how to make money."

"Making money isn't everything," I said.

"Maybe it's not everything," said Dad, "but it's sure way ahead of whatever is in second place."

I sighed. There was no point in arguing with Dad when the subject was money. I lowered my head and fiddled nervously with my notebook.

"Well," said Sarah, finally breaking the silence. She drew in a deep breath and got to her feet. "I guess I should be going."

Poor Sarah. I'd invited her over to help plan for the capture of The Thing, not to witness a family fight. No wonder she was in such a hurry to leave.

"Nice seeing everyone," she said, backing toward the door as she waved good-bye.

"Thanks for coming over, dear," said Mom.

"Wesley seems to like you," said my father, getting to his feet. "That's good."

Sarah blushed.

"See if you can talk some sense into him," he continued. "Get him off this writing thing."

"Yes, sir," said Sarah. She forced a smile, then hurried out the door.

I excused myself and sprinted after her.

"Sarah, I'm sorry you had to sit through that little fight," I said.

"It's all right," she said. A full moon lit the scar

on her chin, played off her round cheeks, and sparkled in her eyes. "It's just that I thought we were going to talk about catching The Thing."

"Do you still want to do it?" I asked.

"Of course, and so does Nick," said Sarah. "He's got big plans for the money. I think he wants to buy a dog farm."

I smiled. "Then let's ride out there again in the morning," I said. "We'll sneak up on The Thing and throw a rope around him before he knows what hit him."

"I wouldn't be so confident," said Sarah. "An operation like that is going to require military precision."

I saluted. "Then you can lead the way, General!"

Sarah saluted back. "By tomorrow night, Sergeant, we're going to be rich."

"When my dad sees all that money, he's going to be so proud of me," I said.

"I don't think you have to get a lot of money to make him proud," said Sarah. She shook her head, tossing her ponytail to the side. "I bet he's proud of you just as you are."

I wished what she said was true, but I knew it wasn't. I suspected Sarah knew it wasn't true, too.

Chapter Six
UNLUCKY DAY

The next morning's paper contained some horrible news. It didn't say that the world was about to end or that a tornado was bearing down on Crimson Beach. The bad news was right at the top of the front page, but it wasn't the headline. It was the date. Friday the thirteenth.

I couldn't have picked a worse day to go on a monster hunt.

Still, a million dollars is a powerful lure. By eight o'clock that morning the three of us were on our bikes and heading for our showdown with the terrible Thing.

The heat that had blistered Crimson Beach for so long had slid off to the south. In its place there was now a crispness in the air that hinted at the coming fall. A half hour later, when we pedaled into Smuggler's Cove, we'd hardly broken a sweat.

After ditching our bikes in the woods, we set out through the brush on tiptoe, hoping to surprise The Thing at breakfast. Or, better yet, in bed.

"I know this isn't a good time to bring this up," whispered Nick from somewhere over my shoulder. "But what's our plan? How are we going to catch this guy?"

I turned and smiled at Nick. As usual, he had Killer tucked under his arm. I tapped my head. "We're going to catch him with superior brains," I said.

"What if he's not that stupid?" said Nick.

Sometimes Nick was such a dolt. "He's The Thing," I said. "How smart can he be?"

"The way I see it, all we've got to do is jump him when he's not looking," whispered Sarah. She was dressed for war: camouflage cap, T-shirt, and pants. "Wesley and I will hold him down. Nick, you tie him up."

"You make it sound so easy," whispered Nick as we skirted a huge boulder.

"It will be," I said, climbing over a fallen tree limb. "Trust me."

"So what are we going to tie him up with?" asked Nick in a high, whiny voice as we stepped through a stand of low brush. "I don't see any rope around here."

I paused in mid-stride. "Uh-oh." I forced a smile and looked at my partners. "I knew I'd forgotten something."

"Oh, great," said Sarah, throwing up her arms. "Now we've got to go all the way back." She shook her head with disgust. "Next time leave the planning to me. I know how to run a military operation."

Nick raised his hand. "I'd be glad to go back home for the rope."

"Thanks, but no thanks," I said. If Nick went home we'd never see him again.

I had to think fast. "Wait a minute. Remember that closet upstairs? We'll lock him in that."

"What if he doesn't want to be locked up?" asked Nick.

"How strong can he be?" I said. "Don't forget. It's three against one."

Nick grumbled something in reply just as we stepped from the woods and into the little clearing around the museum.

"Hold up," said Sarah, raising her hand. "Let's not go rushing in."

Nick squinted up at the old building through

his big, round glasses. "Let's not go in at all," he said.

"We have to go in," said Sarah. "But let's do it so quietly even the walls won't know we've sneaked past."

I glanced up at the old museum. Even in the bright sun it looked like something out of a horror movie. Hunched and broken, with its missing door and shattered windows, it resembled nothing less than a battered skull.

I collected my strength, drew in a deep breath, and stole quietly through the broken doorway. Nick and Sarah followed close behind, on tiptoe.

The big room looked much as it had before. We moved in silence, crossing on cat's paws to the staircase.

"Shhhh!" I said, suddenly freezing. I turned and put a finger to my lips. "Something's upstairs."

Nick gulped. Sarah cupped a hand to her ear and listened.

Clink! "Did you hear that?" I whispered.

Nick had heard it. There couldn't have been any other reason for him to have suddenly pressed himself against the wall.

Sarah swallowed and gave me a look of alarm.

"Let's get out of here," she whispered.

I glanced up at the ceiling. Whatever was making the sound was on the second floor.

Clink! Clink! Clink! The sounds came again, louder this time.

"Maybe it's just the wind banging against an old screen," I suggested hopefully.

"There's no wind," Sarah quickly pointed out.

"And I don't remember any screens," whispered Nick.

Neither did I.

KEE-RACK!

Someone above us had just broken a board.

KEE-RUNCH! Then another.

"That's it!" said Nick, turning to run. "Here comes The Thing!"

"Gangway!" screamed Sarah, sprinting for the door.

"Run for your lives!" I yelled, wheeling about.

Nick had almost made it to safety when suddenly a figure stepped into the doorway, blocking the way.

Chapter Seven
OUTLAWS

The three of us screamed so loud I thought the old building might collapse around us. The figure in the doorway, lit by the sunlight beyond, held its ground.

"Shut up!" it shouted. "Shut up!"

It took us nearly a minute to quiet down. Nick was hugging Killer so hard I thought the stuffing might pop.

"It's . . . it's The Thing," stammered Sarah.

"It's ugly all right, but it's not The Thing," I said, recognizing the person at the door from the silhouette of his derby hat. "It's only Teddy LaBone."

"At your service," said Teddy, lifting his hat in greeting.

For a moment we peered at each other warily, like cats on a fence. Then he snarled and started toward me. "What are you doing here?" he demanded.

"We're . . . we're not doing anything," mumbled Nick. "We came here by accident."

"An accident is just what you're going to have if you stick around," said Teddy. He glanced down at a pretend watch on his wrist. "Isn't it a little past your bedtime?"

"You can't scare us," I said.

"He can't?" muttered Nick, his voice shaking.

"We're not going anywhere," I said. "In fact, you're the one that has to leave."

Teddy raised his fist and stepped toward me, but I wasn't the least bit worried. I knew he'd never risk hitting me. He wouldn't take the chance that one of my slimy pet germs might leap onto his fist.

"We don't have to go anywhere," I said. "For your information, my family owns this place. You're trespassing, mister."

That jarred a laugh out of him. He cupped a hand to his mouth and called up the stairs. "Hey, Will. Pack up your stuff. The owner just kicked us out!"

A moment later Will Pickens came loping down the stairs, a hammer in one hand, a crowbar in the other.

"Hey! What are you guys doing here?" he asked. He tried to scowl, but his rosy cheeks and pearly teeth gave away his naturally happy spirit.

Teddy spit onto the floor. "Wesley Shakespeare says he owns this place. Ain't that funny?" He laughed.

Will waited a second, then laughed, too. "Yeah, Teddy. That's funny all right."

Teddy pointed a gloved finger at my forehead. "Get this, and get it straight," he said. "The Outlaws rule this museum." He slapped his chest. "The Outlaws, that's me and Will."

"We're going to be rich," said Will. He waved the crowbar above his short blond hair. "We've got finders keepers on the diamonds hidden in here."

"Shut up, Will!" yelled Teddy. His eyes filled with fire. "You know, sometimes you're a real blabbermouth."

"What did I say?" said Will, innocent as an angel.

"What diamonds?" I asked. "Everything in this building belongs to me, you know."

Teddy glared at Will. "My partner doesn't know what he's talking about," he said. "There are no diamonds here, are there?"

"But you said that smugglers from Smuggler's Cove might have stashed their—"

"Would you shut your trap!" shouted Teddy.

"So that's why you've been ripping apart the boards upstairs," said Sarah.

"Anything you find is mine," I said. "This place belongs to me and I can prove it."

"We'll get the police," said Nick bravely.

"Go ahead," said Teddy. "By the time the police get around to checking this place out, we'll be long gone."

"We'll be living it up on some tropical beach," said Will. He beamed. "We're going to be rich."

"We're going to be rich, too," I said, raising my chin. "We're going to capture the monster that lives here. The Thing."

"Monster?" said Will. He looked around nervously. "Where? Where?"

I exchanged a worried glance with Sarah. If The Thing was living in the museum, surely Will and Teddy would have seen him by now. Maybe I hadn't seen anything at the window after all.

It was beginning to look more and more like Friday the thirteenth was a bad day for Thing hunting.

"Come on," I said, motioning to Sarah and Nick with my head. "Let's go get the authorities."

"No need for that," came a deep, bullfrog voice. "The authorities are here."

Everyone spun around and looked at the door. We had a visitor.

Chapter Eight

CONDEMNED

"Alan Hammer. City Housing Inspector," said a fat man in a brown uniform, stepping through the door. His face was all red and sweaty and there was a ton of brush and leaves stuck to his uniform.

He wiped his forehead off with the back of his arm and looked around. "It's no wonder this place hasn't been inspected in years. It's harder to get to than the mountains of the moon."

"What are you inspecting it for?" I asked. I stuck out my hand. "Hi. I'm Wesley Shakespeare. My family owns this place."

Mr. Hammer shook my hand, then went around the room shaking everybody else's as well. When he came to Teddy, though, all he got was a wave.

"My, my, my," said the inspector, looking around. "This old place certainly has seen better days, hasn't it?"

65

Everybody nodded their heads in agreement.

Mr. Hammer's eyes fell on Will and his hammer and crowbar.

"It looks as if you kids have been making some repairs," he said. "That's good. Maybe we won't have to burn it after all."

"Burn it!" everyone said at once.

"It's what we do with old buildings like this," explained Mr. Hammer matter-of-factly. He pulled a brown book out of his back pocket and began making notes. "The fire department uses these places for practice."

"But . . . but you just can't burn my family's museum down," I stammered.

"Let's see now, exposed wires, broken boards, missing windows," said Mr. Hammer, furiously writing in his book. "Holes in the walls, garbage on the floor . . ." He closed up his book and sighed. "Let's face it, folks. This place is a mess."

"It won't be for long though," I said. "We're going to fix it up. We're going to get rugs, paint, new windows. You'll see."

Mr. Hammer smiled as if he didn't believe a word I was saying. He looked up at the ceiling. "Let's see what's cooking upstairs, shall we?"

"There's nothing wrong with the upstairs," I said, remembering it from my last visit. "Maybe a little dusty, but that's it."

"Nothing that a broom won't fix!" said Sarah enthusiastically, as if she planned to start sweeping at once.

"Follow me," said Mr. Hammer, starting up the stairs. "If it's as nice as you say, I might just pass this old place."

Like a string of obedient sheep, we followed Mr. Hammer up the stairs to the second floor.

"Oh my," said the inspector when he reached the top of the stairs. "I hope you've got a very special broom."

"What do you mean?" I said, coming up behind him. "Believe me, Mr. Hammer, there's nothing we can't fix. In fact we—" I gasped. "Oh, no!"

The second floor had been destroyed. Since we'd last visited the museum, Will and Teddy had ripped huge holes in the walls and the floor. Bits of splintered lumber lay about like giant toothpicks.

"This place is a disaster," said Mr. Hammer. "Someone could fall into one of those holes in the floor and break a leg. I'm afraid we're going to have to condemn it. It's unfit for human occupancy. Sorry, kids, but she's gotta burn."

"But you can't do that," I said. Without thinking, I grabbed Mr. Hammer by the elbow and turned him around. "We want to make this into a museum again."

Mr. Hammer patted my hand. "Sorry, son. But it looks to me as if it would take at least a thousand dollars to bring this place up to code. All the lumber has to be replaced, those walls have to be patched. You'll need glass for the windows, et cetera, et cetera, et cetera." He raised a single bushy eyebrow. "Do you have that kind of money?"

I shrugged, then turned my pockets inside out. Two paper clips, a pencil, and three pennies came tumbling out. I groaned. "It looks like I'm a little short right now."

"Maybe we can find a way to make the money," suggested Sarah. "We could wash cars or bake cookies or something."

Teddy laughed. "A thousand dollars' worth of cookies? Good luck!"

"You're going to need the cash in a hurry," said Mr. Hammer. "I'll be inspecting again in about ten days."

"Ten days!" I said. "How can we get a thousand dollars in less than two weeks?"

"The fire department has an exercise coming up at the end of the month. I plan to recommend this old building," he said. "Show me you can make it safe and I'll find another place to burn."

"But ten days," I repeated.

He took another look around the room and shook his head. "My, my, my," he muttered. "Someone really vandalized this place. You all deserve a big pat on the back for trying to nail it back together."

"Thank you, sir," said Teddy, tipping his hat.

"We try our best," said Will, waving his crowbar.

"Crimson Beach could use more kids like you," said Mr. Hammer over his shoulder as he started down the stairs. "Believe me, I'm going to be sorry to see your clubhouse burn."

"Yeah, I bet," I muttered, following him to the door.

Just outside the building he turned and waved at us with his brown book.

"Ten days," he said. "Not a minute more."

"Yes, sir," I said, watching him disappear into the woods.

"I can't believe it," said Sarah. "What did we do to deserve such bad luck?"

I didn't have the heart to tell her it was Friday the thirteenth. I kicked at some rocks and then turned angrily to Teddy.

"This is all your fault," I said. "You wrecked my Uncle Max's museum."

"Me?" said Teddy, putting a hand to his chest. "What did I do?"

"What didn't you do?" I said. I reached out to poke him in the nose, but he leapt back as if my finger was spitting germs. "Now you've ruined it for all of us. We can't have the old museum, and you can't have your treasure. Thanks to you, the whole place will be going up in smoke."

Teddy laughed. "Are you kidding? We want a fire."

"What?" said Will.

"I don't get it," said Sarah.

Neither did I, at first. Then, slowly, a terrible truth began to dawn on me. No wonder Teddy was so eager to see the museum burn. Diamonds were the hardest substance in the world. Nothing could destroy them. After the fire was over, all Teddy and Will would have to do was sift through the ashes and fish out the diamonds. It would be like plucking seeds from a melon.

Chapter Nine
SLOPPY SMUGGLERS

I should have stayed in bed. Friday the thirteenth had turned out to be a disaster. Not only did we fail to capture The Thing, but it now looked as if we were going to lose the museum as well.

We walked back through the woods at the pace of a funeral procession.

"That poor museum," I said, as I shuffled down the trail behind Sarah and Nick. "How can they burn it? They'll be destroying history."

"They might be destroying The Thing, too," said Nick. He held back a branch and let his sister pass. "Don't they realize there might be a monster living in there?"

"They don't care," I said bitterly. "They don't care about anything."

"I care," said Nick softly. "I was thinking that

maybe The Thing could be my pet." He looked back at his sister. "Of course only if he doesn't bite."

Sarah rubbed the scar on her chin and smiled. "I don't know what Mom and Dad would say about having a Thing in the house."

"All they said was that I couldn't have a dog," replied Nick. He hugged Killer. "They didn't say anything about monsters."

We all laughed. We were still laughing when we emerged from the woods and onto the rock and sand parking lot at the edge of Smuggler's Cove. The place was as deserted as before. Only the cries of the sea gulls overhead and the sounds of the waves crashing along the shoreline interrupted the silence.

I gazed out beyond the waves, far out to the gray horizon, and sighed. What was wrong with me? I'd wasted everybody's day chasing a dream. I guess it was the writer in me who was to blame, the one with the wild imagination. The one who believed in amusement parks, and monsters called The Thing, and in that faraway day when a silly dreamer like Wesley Shakespeare would become a world-famous writer.

I glanced down at the ground and kicked at the sand. Why did I have to be such a fool!

I kicked again, sending up a spray of sand, rocks, shells, and—I couldn't believe my eyes—diamonds!

I gasped, dropped to one knee, and scooped up a handful of sand.

"D-d-diamonds!" I stammered, looking down at a fortune in sparkling jewels nestled among the sand and shells. My Adam's apple started bobbing up and down like a yo-yo on fast forward. "C-c-come quick! We're rich!"

Nick and Sarah came running.

I held out my hand. "Look what I just uncovered!"

Sarah and Nick crowded around my shaking hand like flies swarming to honey.

"He's right!" said Nick. He plucked a tiny diamond from my hand and held it to the light. "We must have just found where the smugglers buried their treasure."

I looked back toward the museum and chuckled. "Wait till Teddy and Will find out they've been looking in the wrong place."

Sarah bent down and picked more diamonds out of the sand.

"Are you sure these are real diamonds?" she said. "They look kind of fake to me."

I clucked my tongue. "You are always so negative," I said. "For once, would you just trust me?"

"It just seems crazy," said Sarah. "Why would all these diamonds be lying around down here? Why weren't they buried in a treasure chest?"

I rolled my eyes. "Sometimes you are so dumb," I said. I scooped up another handful of sand and shells and picked out three more diamonds. "Don't you get it? We're dealing with a gang of sloppy smugglers."

"Sloppy smugglers?" said Nick. He was on his hands and knees, too, picking up more of the sparkling jewels.

"Smugglers have been coming into Smuggler's Cove for hundreds of years," I said. "Some of them probably spilled their treasure along the way."

Nick looked up and grinned. "Sure. That makes sense."

"Of course it does," I said. I reached out and tapped Sarah on her freckled nose. "I just made you rich, my friend. You should thank me."

"I'll thank you when we sell the diamonds," said Sarah. "That is, *if* they're diamonds."

"Oh, they're diamonds, all right," I said. "And I can prove it."

"You can not," said Sarah.

"Diamonds are the hardest substance there is," I said, picking up the last sparkling jewel from the sand. "It's a well-known fact that diamonds can cut glass."

"So?" said Sarah.

"So I'll show you," I said, leading everyone over to our bikes.

Sarah grumbled and followed.

"Watch this," I said, taking hold of the mirror attached to the handlebars on my bike. "Every jeweler in the world knows this trick."

I took one of the tiny diamonds and drew it across the mirror. *Scrrr-atch!* It left a mark from one side to the other, clear as if it had been drawn in ink.

"Wow!" said Nick.

"I told you so," I said.

Sarah wet her finger, then rubbed it across the scratch. It stayed. "Well, maybe you are right," she said. "It definitely left a mark."

I looked around nervously, then shoved the diamonds deep into my pocket. "I suggest we get these down to Mr. Hook at the Crimson Beach

Jewelry Shop. He's got a big safe down there."

Nick put his diamonds into his pocket. "Let's go," he said, strapping Killer onto his bike rack, then climbing on. "I don't want to get robbed."

We rode most of the way to town in silence. All of us were lost in thoughts of what we were going to do with our new-found riches.

The way I figured it, we must have had at least a million dollars in diamonds in our pockets. With my share I'd buy a printing press and start making books. Before long everyone in the world would be reading my stories. I'd be on all the talk shows, my picture would be in the papers, and there would be a whole series of movies about my incredible life. Naturally, I'd also give lots of money to charity.

When we finally walked into the Crimson Beach Jewelry Shop, I half expected the clerks to come running out for my autograph.

"Wow," said Nick, looking at all the watches and jewels in the shop's shiny display cases. "They've got almost as many diamonds in this store as we have in our pockets."

"Almost," I said with a wink.

The owner of the store, Mr. Hook, was standing in the back talking to a woman in a feathered hat. "That's who we want to see," I said, turning to Sarah. "He's the man with the money."

Sarah looked up at the fancy chandeliers on the ceiling and forced a smile. She still didn't seem convinced that we were on the verge of incredible wealth.

"Ahem," I said, loudly clearing my throat. "Mr. Hook, could we talk to you for a minute?"

Mr. Hook and the woman both turned. Mr. Hook rubbed his short gray beard and looked the three of us up and down. "You'll have to wait a minute. Can't you see? I'm busy with a customer," he said sharply.

I chuckled and reached into my pocket. "Get rid of her," I said. I drew out a fistful of diamonds and opened my hand. "We're here to talk business."

Mr. Hook furrowed his brow. The woman looked at me as if I was crazy.

"Look!" said Nick excitedly, pulling a handful of diamonds out of his own pocket. "I've got some, too!"

Mr. Hook looked at us. "Is this a joke?" he asked.

"No, sir," I said, spilling diamonds onto the

counter. "We're here to sell them for a million dollars."

"A million dollars," repeated Nick, in case Mr. Hook hadn't heard. "They scratch glass and everything. We tested them."

"Everything scratches glass, including glass," said Mr. Hook. He picked up one of the diamonds and held it up to the light. "Where did you find these anyway, in a parking lot?"

Despite myself, I gasped. "How did you know?"

"Where else would you find broken windshield glass?" he said. "Sorry, kids. I can't give you a million dollars for broken car glass." He waved his hand over the counter. "I can't even give you a penny."

For a moment I thought I might faint. I'd done it again, let my imagination run wild.

"But . . . but it scratched glass," said Nick. He looked around, stunned and confused.

"I told you so," said Sarah, glaring. Her face was as red as the carpet on the floor of the Crimson Beach Jewelry Shop.

I gave Mr. Hook a wave and a big fake smile and began backing out of the store. "Come on," I said between clenched teeth. "Time to go."

Nick scratched at his short hair and wrinkled

his face. "But I thought you said that if it scratched—"

"Nick, let's get out of here," said Sarah, grabbing her brother by the shoulder and spinning him around. "Get it through your head! There are no diamonds."

"There aren't?" he whined, hurrying alongside his sister. "You mean we're not going to get a million dollars?"

"Sorry," I said, as we scurried out the door. "We're not going to get any money. In fact, we're not going to get anything."

"No, that's not entirely true," said Sarah. She stopped on the sidewalk and put her face right up against my nose. "Actually, thanks to you, we did get something in there."

"We did?" I said, staring down my nose at her, cross-eyed. "What did we get in there?"

"Embarrassed," said Sarah.

Chapter Ten

A GREAT IDEA

At the breakfast table on Saturday morning I told my father all about our meeting with the building inspector.

"So if we don't get a thousand dollars in the next ten days, they'll burn down the museum," I said, gesturing with a spoonful of corn flakes.

"Uh-huh, very interesting," muttered Dad. He was completely invisible behind his newspaper, *The Wall Street Journal.*

"So I was thinking," I said, nervously clearing my throat. "Umm, maybe you could give us a thousand dollars. After all, it's your museum, too."

My father's black, slicked-down hair and thin, hawk-nosed face suddenly appeared over the top of the paper. He raised an eyebrow. "Did I just hear you say you wanted a thousand dollars?"

"To rescue the Oddity Museum," I said. I'd put on a tie over my Shakespeare T-shirt again. I was hoping to impress my father. "The city wants to burn it down. They claim it's unfit for humans."

"It was unfit for humans the day it opened," said Dad coldly. He dropped the newspaper onto the table. "There's no money in a museum. Never has been, never will be. I say, let it burn!"

"But Dad—" I protested.

"Go into banking, discover gold, or write a best-selling play," said my father. "That's how you get rich."

"But I don't want to be rich," I said. "I just . . ." My voice trailed off. The conversation was over. Dad had once again raised the paper and vanished into the financial pages of *The Wall Street Journal*.

I spent the rest of breakfast in silence, thinking. Dad may not have given me any money, but he had given me something nearly as good: an idea. "You get rich by writing a best-selling play," he had said. I was going to do just that!

After breakfast I took a walk through town, letting my thoughts percolate. I was surprised at how quickly the elements of the story began to fall into place. A farmer would discover The

Thing living in his barn. Then he would call in the army to capture it. I didn't have an ending yet, but I'd figure out something when I got there. First things first, I thought.

I was writing down my ideas for the play when I spotted Sarah and Nick through the window of Burger World. They were sitting in a booth, eating their lunch. I don't think they saw me till I came blasting through the front door.

"Guess what!" I shouted from the other side of the restaurant. "We're putting on a play!"

Nick looked up, a French fry half in, half out of his mouth. Killer was sitting next to him.

I wove my way quickly through the crowded room, shouting all the while. "It's going to be the best play ever! We'll call it 'The Thing Upstairs'!"

"Wesley, calm down," said Sarah. A root beer and a hamburger sat before her on the table. "There's no need to yell."

"We're going to be rich," I said, grabbing a handful of Nick's French fries as I swung into their booth. "The play is going to be all about that creature that haunts the museum." I shoved the fries into my mouth and went on without chewing. "We'll put it on next Saturday at the museum," I mumbled. "We'll charge four dollars to get in. If 250 people show up, we'll make a thousand dollars!"

Sarah whistled. "I don't know. That's a lot of people."

"Maybe we could charge $250," said Nick. "Then we'd only need to sell four tickets."

I rolled my eyes toward the ceiling, then grabbed Sarah's root beer and chugged half of it down in one giant gulp.

"Get this," I said, wiping my mouth with my arm. "The three of us will do everything. We'll make the posters. We'll sell the tickets. We'll be the actors. We'll do it all!"

"What's the play going to be about?" asked Nick.

"I already told you. It's about The Thing Upstairs," I said.

"I know, but what's the story?" said Nick.

I pulled out my notebook, wet my finger, and quickly searched the pages till I found the day's notes.

"It's about a farmer—that's me—a soldier—Sarah—and The Thing—you."

"I'm The Thing?" said Nick. He shivered.

"Remember that monkey suit you wore last Halloween?" I said, leaning across the table.

Nick nodded.

"It will make a perfect Thing outfit," I said. "Isn't this great! We already have our costumes!"

"Costumes are just one part of the play," said Sarah. "What's the story going to be about?"

I grabbed Sarah's hamburger and took a bite.

"Ummm," I said, chewing.

"What's it going to be about?" repeated Sarah.

"About a farmer, a soldier, and a Thing," I mumbled, still chewing. "I just told you that."

Sarah looked down at the remains of her hamburger and sighed. "Does it, at least, have a good ending?"

I raised my hand. "Trust me," I mumbled, losing half the hamburger as I spoke. "It's going to have a great ending."

Sarah leveled a finger at my nose. "You can't just say 'The end' in the middle of the story, you know."

"I know," I said. "Believe me, this play is going to have the best ending ever."

Sarah grumbled.

"Hey, I'm a writer, aren't I? Writers write endings." I grabbed another handful of fries and stuffed them into my mouth.

"Hey, that's my lunch," said Nick.

"I know we can get people to come," I said between chews. "All we've got to do is come up with a great advertising poster."

Sarah narrowed her eyes and studied me long and hard. "Are you really going to have a good ending? Tell me the truth now."

"I'm telling you the truth," I said, looking her straight in the eye. "I'm going to have a great ending. I promise."

Sarah nodded. "If that promise is real, then I can get people to the show."

"You can?" I said, sitting back.

"I'll make up the posters myself," said Sarah. "This is just like a military operation. It takes planning and execution."

"It does?" I said, surprised.

"Yep. We can't lose," said Sarah.

I grinned. Sarah was practically guaranteeing we'd make the money we needed to save the museum. To celebrate, I finished off her root beer, set down the cup, and let out a tremendous belch. "Wow. Am I ever feeling good."

"You're going to feel even better when you see my signs," said Sarah.

"What will they say?" I asked.

"Let me surprise you," said Sarah.

Chapter Eleven
SURPRISED

On Sunday afternoon I discovered Sarah and Nick tacking up a poster on the telephone pole outside of Reisman's Bagel Shop.

"Ta-da!" sang Sarah when she saw me coming. "We just put up our last poster. Every telephone pole, vacant wall, and store window in town is now advertising our play."

She tapped the poster, stood back, and beamed, like a proud mother showing off her new baby. "So, what do you think?"

I grinned and looked up and down the street. I was famous! My play was up in lights, so to speak.

"Thanks, Sarah," I said. I put my nose up to the poster and read the words. This is what it said:

DON'T MISS THE
CRIMSON BEACH PLAYERS IN
THE THING UPSTAIRS!

THE THING UPSTAIRS

a new play by W. Shakespeare
Saturday at noon
At the Wonderland Oddity Museum
behind Smuggler's Cove
—Just Four Dollars—

This play has the greatest ending of all time. If you are not completely surprised we'll give you DOUBLE your money back!

I gulped. "Double your money back?"

Sarah tipped her army cap. "That was my idea," she said proudly. "People would be fools not to come to a show with a guarantee like that."

"People would be fools to offer a guarantee like that," I mumbled in reply. I swallowed and felt a sudden quiver in my knees. "What if the ending isn't that good?"

Nick tilted his head. "But it will be. You promised."

I forced a smile. Beads of sweat erupted on my forehead.

"This play was your idea," said Sarah, narrowing her eyes. "I expect you to carry through, soldier!"

"Umm, maybe there's more than one way to make that thousand dollars." I snapped my fingers. "I know! We'll capture The Thing and sell him to the zoo."

"There is no Thing, remember?" said Sarah. "And even if there was, we probably couldn't capture him in time."

Nick put a hand to his mouth. "I just thought of something awful. What if The Thing is hidden somewhere in the museum? If there's a fire he'll die." He sniffled. "How can The Thing be my pet if he's burned to a crisp?"

Sarah put a hand on her little brother's shoulder. "Don't worry. There isn't going to be any fire. Our play is going to save the museum."

Just then Mrs. Reisman stepped out of her bagel shop and saw our new poster.

"The Crimson Beach Players in a new play by W. Shakespeare!" she said. "I love William Shakespeare."

"Well," I said quickly. "Actually, the W stands for—"

"And double your money back if the ending doesn't surprise you," Mrs. Reisman went on. She had a bagel in one hand and a smudge of

89

cream cheese on her nose. "My goodness, that's certainly a good deal."

"Does that mean you're coming?" asked Sarah.

"Are you kidding? I'm bringing the whole family." Mrs. Reisman sighed and stared off into the distance, dreaming. "At last, a decent theater has opened in Crimson Beach."

"Whoa, wait a minute," I said. "The W doesn't—"

"Shakespeare. The greatest playwright of all time," said Mrs. Reisman. She held aloft her bagel. "He wrote so many great plays. I think my favorite is still 'Much Ado About Nothing.' Is that the one you're doing?"

"No," said Nick. "We're doing 'The Thing Upstairs.'"

"That's not a Shakespeare play I'm familiar with," said Mrs. Reisman.

"Don't worry," I muttered. "'The Thing Upstairs' just might turn out to be much ado about nothing anyway."

Chapter Twelve

THE BEAUTIFUL MISERABLE DAY

Me and my big mouth. How was I ever going to come up with the greatest surprise ending of all time? I didn't even know how to write the worst ending of all time.

On Monday I went to work. Right after breakfast I sat down at my desk, took out my pencil and my notebook, and began to write "The Thing Upstairs."

"Once upon a time a horrible Thing lived upstairs," I wrote at the top of the first page.

I sat back in my chair and grinned. "What a great beginning," I told myself. "Maybe this won't be such a hard play to write after all."

I turned in my chair and stared out the window. "Now what's going to come next?" I thought.

Outside the window I could see cars passing on the street. Daniel Bick came riding by on his bicycle. Jesse Wheeler's cat chased a squirrel up a tree. Lots of things were happening outside. Unfortunately, nothing was happening inside my head.

When lunchtime came I went downstairs and made a tuna sandwich, ate it slowly, and read the newspaper.

"Maybe I can get an idea from the newspaper," I thought.

I read stories about the auto show, about a flood, and about the new school budget. None of the stories had anything to do with Things living upstairs.

When I trudged back to my room after lunch I was as lost as ever.

All afternoon I read my opening sentence over and over and over. "Once upon a time a horrible Thing lived upstairs."

But try as I might, I couldn't think what happened next.

By four o'clock I was exhausted from doing nothing and so I quit work for the day.

At dinner that night I was served rice, burritos, and embarrassing questions.

"How is your play coming?" asked Mom, scooping some rice onto my plate.

"Ummm, okay, I guess," I said, staring into my food.

"I've seen posters all over town advertising your famous surprise ending," said Dad. He leaned across the table and lowered his voice. "Mind telling us what it is? I promise not to tell."

I put a fork into my rice and swirled it around. "I . . . I haven't gotten there yet," I mumbled.

"You don't know the ending yet?" said Dad. He formed his black eyebrows into a sharp V. "I suggest you come up with something fast. You promised double your money back. Good heavens, son, you could lose a fortune."

"Don't worry, Dad," I said. "I'll think up something."

"I always said you couldn't make a living as a writer," he grumbled. "But I never thought it could actually cost you money. What kind of a job is that?"

I sighed and lowered my head.

"Now, now," said Mom. She reached over and patted my hand. "You're a good writer. I'm sure you'll come up with a terrific ending."

"Sure," I said, looking up. I gave her a half smile. "Maybe tomorrow."

But when tomorrow was over I was still stuck

on the first line, "Once upon a time a horrible Thing lived upstairs."

On Wednesday I took my pencil and my notebook and left the house early. It was another beautiful summer day. There were blue skies above, the smell of flowers in the air, and the sounds of songbirds in the trees. All in all, it was very depressing.

"How can I think up a horror story on such a beautiful day?" I thought. I looked up at the perfect, cloudless sky and very nearly burst into tears. "Why is the world against me?" I yelled.

Aimlessly I walked through town, hoping that inspiration would come to me.

Unfortunately, inspiration never did catch up with me. But Sarah and Nick did, on the sidewalk outside the post office.

"There you are," shouted Sarah, angrily stomping my way. "Where have you been hiding? We've been looking for you since yesterday."

"Hi," I said, waving.

"We have to rehearse," said Nick. He squinted up at me through his big round glasses. His flattop looked limp and tired. So did Killer, dangling by a single leg from Nick's hand. "Did you forget? The play is on Saturday."

"I didn't forget," I said. "I've been busy writing." I held up my notebook and my pencil. "See?"

"Good," said Sarah. "Let's go back to my house for a rehearsal."

"I don't think that would be a very good idea," I said.

"You don't think we need to rehearse?" said Sarah. "How can we put on a play if we don't practice?"

"We can't," I said. "It's just that . . ." I lowered my head and kicked at some pebbles on the sidewalk. "It's just that I . . ."

"That you don't have a great ending," said Sarah, finishing my sentence.

"No, it's not that," I said, looking up.

"Whew," said Sarah, wiping her arm across her brow. "For a minute there I was afraid you were stuck on the ending."

"The ending isn't my problem," I said quietly, looking down at my notebook. The problem wasn't the ending. It was the second line of the play. But I couldn't tell that to Nick and Sarah. They'd kill me.

Luckily, I was saved by Will Pickens and Teddy LaBone, who chose that very moment to stroll around the corner. Teddy was carrying a plastic grocery bag in his gloved hand, and Will was holding a hammer.

"Well, if it isn't the litterbugs," said Teddy, raising his derby hat with his free hand. "You're lucky we decided to clean up after you."

"You guys just had a very close call," said Will. His round, rosy cheeks glowed like ripe peaches. "If it wasn't for us, you three would be on your way to jail."

"Jail?" said Nick. He looked around nervously as if expecting a police raid. "What did we do?"

"We didn't do a thing," said Sarah. "We're not litterbugs."

Teddy reached into his plastic bag and fished out a handful of papers. "Not litterbugs! Then what do you call these?"

Sarah and Nick gasped. Teddy was holding the play posters, the ones they'd put up on Sunday.

"Somebody scattered these all over town," said Teddy. "They were littering walls and poles and the insides of store windows everywhere."

Will laughed. "I think we got them all, thank goodness."

Teddy looked us each in the eye. "Well, aren't you going to thank us?"

I made a fist and snarled.

"I suggest you put those back where you found them," said Sarah. She made two fists and shook them in Teddy's face. He stepped back, probably more fearful of her germs than her punch.

"You just don't want anyone to come to our play," said Nick. He made a little fist and shook it alongside his head like a tambourine. "That's why you tore down our posters."

"Duh," said Teddy. He laughed.

"We'll put the posters back up," said Sarah, sticking out her scarred chin.

"And we'll tear them right back down," said Teddy.

"It's not fair," said Nick. He sniffled and ran his arm under his nose. "Wesley just wrote a story with the biggest surprise ending ever."

"Oh, yeah?" sneered Teddy.

"He's got the whole thing written down in his book," said Nick.

Teddy eyed my notebook. "Is that right? It's all in there, huh?"

"Yep," said Nick. He held up Killer. "The ending is such a secret even my puppy and I don't know what it is."

"Is that so?" said Teddy.

"That's so," said Nick, wiggling Killer in Will's face.

Suddenly, Teddy's hand shot out like a snake's tongue.

"Hey!" I shouted. "What are you doing?"

Wham! Before I knew what had hit me, he'd grabbed my notebook and taken off down the street as if rocket propelled.

"See you later!" he yelled over his shoulder.

Will leapt into the air like a poked rabbit and lit out after his partner. "Teddy! Wait for me!"

"Give me that book!" I shouted, too stunned to move. By the time I finally collected myself, they had already rounded the corner and disappeared.

"Now we're really in trouble," said Sarah. "They'll soon know the ending to the play. Then they'll blab it all over town and ruin the surprise."

"I don't think so," I said. "When they open my book they'll discover the surprise is on them."

"Huh? What do you mean?" asked Sarah.

"Nothing," I said. That was also what Teddy and Will were about to discover inside the notebook.

Chapter Thirteen
DOUBLE TROUBLE

I awoke on Friday sweating, but not because it was hot. In fact, the day had dawned cloudy and cool. I was sweating because there was only one day left till I met my doom.

"Maybe I'll get lucky," I thought, staring up at the ceiling. "Maybe no one will come to the play."

The more I thought of this, the more likely it seemed. Perhaps Teddy and Will had actually done me a huge favor by tearing down our posters. If no one knew about the play, then no one would come.

Of course I didn't want to see the old museum burned, but why should I have to be humiliated in front of everyone in the bargain?

I was awakened from this fantasy by a shout outside my window.

"Wesley! Get up! Time to rehearse!"

I crawled out of bed, shuffled to the window, and moaned. It was Sarah and Nick. Both of them were ready for the play. Sarah was wearing her father's too-big army uniform and Nick was dressed up in the monkey suit left over from last Halloween.

"Hurry up! Put on your farmer costume! We'll rehearse back at our house!" yelled Sarah. She was looking up with her hands cupped around her mouth. "Let's go, soldier! Let's go!"

I gave them a halfhearted wave, then fell back into bed. I wasn't about to go outside for a rehearsal. There was nothing to rehearse.

"Wessss-leee!" I heard Sarah shout.

I put the pillow over my head and went back to sleep.

Fifteen minutes later Sarah and Nick were standing in my room. "Your mother let us in," said Nick.

Sarah leaned over and yelled like an army sergeant. "Get up! Get up! Rise and shine, soldier. There's work to do!"

"But I—"

"No excuses," barked Sarah. "I know that Teddy stole your notebook, but I'm sure you can still remember most of it."

In truth, I could remember all of it. "Once upon a time a horrible Thing lived upstairs." But I didn't dare tell that to Sarah.

"We'll be outside waiting," said Sarah. She snapped her fingers. "Move it!"

I groaned, sat up, and rubbed the sleep from my eyes.

"Don't take forever," said Sarah, following her monkey-suited brother out the door. "The play is tomorrow at noon."

I splashed some water on my face, pulled on my farmer costume—a pair of overalls and a wide-brimmed straw hat—and went downstairs.

"Practice makes perfect," said Mom, holding the front door open. "The more you rehearse, the better you're going to be tomorrow."

"But Mom—"

"Even the greatest writers have to go over their stories, writing and rewriting till they get them just right," she said. "I don't care how good your play is, you have to go over it till it's perfect."

"Yes, Mom," I muttered, stepping through the door.

The army sergeant and the monkey were waiting at the top of the steps.

"Guess what!" said Nick, grabbing my elbow. "Teddy and Will put our posters back up."

"They did?" I said, tipping back my hat. "Why did they do that?"

"Maybe Teddy's conscience got to him," said Nick.

"Most unlikely," I said. "Outlaws don't have a conscience."

"The best part is that the posters are back," said Sarah. "Now everyone in town will know about the play."

"Darn! I was hoping no one would show up," I muttered.

"What?" said Sarah.

"Nothing," I said.

"Are we going to practice?" asked Nick. "I don't want anyone to see me standing around in this costume."

"Me neither," said Sarah, looking around. "Come on. Let's go across the street. We can practice in our garage."

"Wait a minute," I said. "I've got something to say."

The time had come to be honest. I had to tell them there was no play. The museum was going to burn with The Thing in it and the Outlaws were going to get their diamonds. The truth wasn't going to be easy. But it was the right thing to do.

"What's the matter?" asked Nick.

I lowered my head and studied the lawn.

"Go on," said Sarah. "We're all friends. Friends share their feelings."

"Well," I began. "You see I had some—"

HONK! HONK! HONK!

I looked up. A carload of kids pulled over to the curb. The driver was leaning on the horn and his passengers were leaning out the windows. I didn't recognize any of them, but they seemed to know who we were.

"Hey! We're all coming to the play tomorrow!" yelled one of the kids. "I hope you guys are rich!"

The three of us—the farmer, the soldier, and the monkey—stared back in silence.

"Teddy and Will said you're going to pay everyone four dollars for coming to the play!" shouted the driver. "I'm inviting all my friends and relatives so you better have lots of money ready."

"You got it all wrong," said Sarah, shouting back. "You have to pay us four dollars to see the play."

"But you have to double our money if the ending isn't a huge surprise. Right?" said the driver.

"Yeah, so?" said Sarah. She put her hand on my shoulder. "W. Shakespeare here has written an ending that's going to surprise your socks off."

"No, he hasn't," said one of the boys in the back seat. "Teddy told us all about the play. So we already know what's going to happen."

"Uh-oh," said Nick. "He found out all about the play from your notebook."

"See you monkeys tomorrow at noon!" shouted the driver. He honked the horn again, then drove away, laughing.

"No wonder Teddy and Will put those posters up again," I said.

"They don't want us to make enough money to save the museum," said Nick.

"It's worse than that," said Sarah. "If we have to give everyone double their money back, we could lose more than a thousand dollars."

Nick gulped. "But we don't have a thousand dollars."

"If we don't keep our promise we could go to jail," I said. I shook my head. "I'm sorry, everybody. This is all my fault. I'm the one who got us into this mess."

Sarah and Nick looked at me as if they couldn't have agreed more.

"The way I see it, we have no choice," said Sarah.

"You're right. We have to call off the play," I said, smiling.

"We're going to do nothing of the sort," said Sarah. She poked me in the chest. "Where's your spirit, soldier?"

"Huh?" I said.

"This is the time to fight, not to run!" she said, giving me another poke. I backed up a step, but she kept on coming. "Get back in your house and write a new ending. Everybody is going to be expecting one thing, so we'll give them something else. If that isn't a surprise, then I don't know what is."

"What a great idea," said Nick.

"Can you do it, Wesley?" said Sarah. "Can you come up with an ending even better than your last one?"

"No problem," I said. And that was the truth.

Chapter Fourteen
PLAY DAY

I stayed up till midnight working on the play. As it turned out, things went better than they had before. Instead of one line, I wrote three.

"Once upon a time a horrible Thing lived upstairs. Some said The Thing was a monster. Some said The Thing was a zombie, half living, half dead."

I was off to a good start. It was too bad the play was going to begin in just a few hours. If I had a few more months, I probably could have finished it.

Around ten o'clock Nick and Sarah came over carrying their costumes. We went into the living room, being careful not to disturb Dad, who was sitting on the couch buried behind the latest issue of *Money* magazine.

"We'll have to rehearse once we get to the museum," said Sarah. She raised an eyebrow. "I hope your new ending is a real shocker."

"The whole play is a shocker," I said. "Believe me, you'll be stunned when you find out what I've written."

"Is it scary?" asked Nick.

"To me it is," I said, imagining what Sarah and Nick were going to do to me when they found out I'd only written three sentences.

"I hope it doesn't scare me too much," said Nick. He hugged Killer to his chest and shivered. "Otherwise I might not be able to speak my lines."

"Don't worry about speaking your lines," I said. To myself I muttered, "No problem, Nick. You have no lines."

"Is your dad going?" asked Sarah, gesturing toward my father.

"I don't know," I said. "As you can see, he's kind of busy."

I watched my dad reading about money and sighed. I really wished that he would take an interest in my writing, but not today. The play was going to be a horrible flop. I didn't want him to see me fail.

Just then a car honked outside and Nick ran to the window.

"It's Mom," he said. "She's ready to drive us to the museum."

"Hurry up, go get your costume," said Sarah.

For a moment I thought about telling Nick and Sarah the truth. But then, just as quickly, I dismissed the thought. It was too late for the truth. People were already on their way to the play. There was no way we could call off the performance now.

I let out a little moan, then went upstairs and got into my farmer's costume.

When I came back downstairs Sarah was talking to my father about the Oddity Museum.

"No, sir, it's not as bad as you think," I heard her say.

Before my father could reply, Sarah's mom honked again.

"Time to go," said Nick, opening the door.

"See you, Mr. Shakespeare," said Sarah.

"See you, Dad," I said.

"Good luck," he replied. "I'll keep my fingers crossed that you don't lose a fortune."

"Thanks for the help," I said, rolling my eyes.

Then out the door we went, one after another,

heading toward what I knew was certain disaster.

Sarah and Nick kept up a steady stream of chatter all the way to the museum, but I wasn't listening. My mind was too busy writing a play complete with the greatest ending in the world.

"Wesley!"

"Huh?" I said.

Sarah poked me in the ribs. "You haven't heard a thing I've said."

I lifted the corner of my big straw hat. "What did you say?"

"I said tell us the story of 'The Thing Upstairs.'"

"Oh, the play, sure," I said. "Ummm. Where should I begin?"

"Begin at the beginning," said Sarah. "That's where most people start."

At that moment the car rounded a corner and there we were at the Smuggler's Cove parking lot.

"Oh, my gosh!" we all exclaimed at once.

It looked like the Crimson Beach Players were a success already. The parking lot was packed. There must have been at least fifty cars crammed into the dirt lot. Six people had just gotten out of a van in front of us, and I could see others heading into the woods toward the museum.

"Looks like you're going to make that thousand dollars easy," said Mrs. Hawkins, parking the car. "Everybody in town must be here."

My heart leapt into my throat. I was a goner. So was the museum. Nick and Sarah were goners, too. They just didn't realize it yet.

"I bet there haven't been this many people at the cove since the smugglers first landed here," said Nick. "It must have taken tons of them to haul all those diamonds and jewels ashore."

"What are you talking about?" said Mrs. Hawkins, getting out of the car. "There never have been any smugglers here. Not a one."

"How can that be?" said Sarah. "It's called Smuggler's Cove."

"Smuggler's Cove was named after Lucinda Smuggler," said Sarah's mom. "She was the first mayor of Crimson Beach. I thought everyone knew that."

"What?" I said, half in, half out of the car. "You mean smugglers didn't land here and hide their diamonds?"

Mrs. Hawkins smiled. "Lucinda Smuggler had a house out here over a hundred years ago. She wasn't a rich lady. I doubt if she ever owned any diamonds."

"Well, isn't that something," I said. "Looks like Teddy and Will have been ripping up that place for nothing."

Nick laughed. "I can hardly wait to tell them they've been wasting their time."

"Fools," I said. "How could anyone believe someone would just leave their diamonds lying around?" I laughed.

"Yeah," said Sarah sarcastically. "How could anyone fall for that old diamond trick?"

She laughed as my face turned red.

"Ahem," I said, clearing my throat. "Don't you think we better get going?"

"Oooh, look," said Sarah, picking up a piece of broken glass. "Diamonds!"

"Very funny," I said, as we headed into the woods behind a pair of football players I recognized from the high school. With them to clear the way, the walk through the tangled woods turned into a stroll down a garden path. Sarah and Nick couldn't stop talking about the fake diamonds. Every time they spotted a piece of broken glass they'd cry out, "Treasure! We're rich!"

They were having a great time making me miserable. Actually, I was doing a pretty good job making myself miserable. I was heading for humiliation and bankruptcy and maybe even jail.

These dreary thoughts dogged me all the way to the museum, where a huge crowd was awaiting the arrival of the Crimson Beach Players.

"They're here!" someone shouted as we stepped from the woods. "There are the people who are going to double our money!"

I gulped and looked around. There must have been at least a hundred people standing around in the weeds, many of whom I recognized. Mrs. Reisman from the bagel shop was there with her family. Mr. Cole, the biology teacher at the high school, was near the doorway talking to Dr. Brown, who worked at the Crimson Beach Natural History Museum. Even the city building inspector, Mr. Hammer, had chosen to attend. He was leaning against a tree, eating a donut.

Lots of kids were there too, including the boy who had stopped his car in front of my house the day before.

"Hey! Where's your sackful of money?" he called.

I forced a smile and waved, pretending not to hear.

"I told you they would show up," yelled someone from the back of the crowd.

"I thought for sure they'd chicken out," said someone else.

I looked around for Teddy and Will, but I didn't see them. They were probably on their way. I couldn't imagine they would miss the opportunity to see me humiliated in public.

Sarah moved to the door of the museum and raised her hand for quiet.

"The play starts in half an hour," she said. "There are no chairs so you'll have to sit on the floor. The price is four dollars. You can pay us as you go in."

Sarah and Nick excused themselves for a minute, leaving me in charge of collecting the money.

"We're going to change into our costumes," said Sarah, leading her brother upstairs.

"Hurry back!" I said.

"We will," said Sarah, as they disappeared into the crowd.

Nearly every person who paid asked me about our double-your-money-back guarantee.

"I plan to collect every penny of it," said a big, barrel-chested man with a tangled black beard that covered half his face. He snorted and looked me over as if expecting to have me for lunch. "I'm a gold miner from Alaska and I've been jumped by everything from a flash flood to a grizzly. I'm not easy to surprise, young fella. If your ending isn't a real knockout, get ready to hand me my eight dollars."

"We're going to try our best," I said, taking his money and stuffing it into a paper sack that served as our cash register.

He pressed his huge face up against my nose. "Your best better be good enough!"

"It will be," I said out loud. "It won't be," I said to myself.

Chapter Fifteen

DISAPPEARED

I stood at the door for nearly half an hour, taking in money by the fistful. Three hundred people must have paid me for the show. We were making a fortune.

The only question was whether we'd get to keep it.

Actually, that wasn't the only question. I did have one other.

Where were Sarah and Nick?

They'd been gone for nearly half an hour. How long could it take to climb into an army uniform and a monkey suit?

If they didn't hurry back I might have to go on without them.

I shivered at the thought and looked around the room. Every inch was filled with theater-goers. Some folks were leaning up against the walls. The rest were seated on the dusty floor, talking among themselves. It sounded a lot like the cafeteria at school, though it didn't smell nearly as awful.

As far as I could tell, my partners weren't anywhere in the room. Grabbing the bag of money, I stepped outside and looked for them there.

"Sarah! Nick!" I yelled over and over as I circled the building.

By the time I'd gotten back inside, it was noon. The crowd was beginning to grow restless.

"Hey! Start the show!" someone yelled.

"This floor is hard!" yelled someone else. "On with the play!"

I gave the audience a half-hearted wave and dashed up the stairs three steps at a time.

"Nick! Sarah!" I shouted. "Where are you?"

But when I reached the top step I could see at once that the second floor was deserted. Anyway, the damaged room hardly looked like the kind of place Nick and Sarah would have chosen to change clothes.

Downstairs, the crowd was growing restless.

"The play! The play! The play!" they began to chant.

If I'd been outside I would have streaked for home, but I was trapped. I had nowhere to go but down.

I drew in a deep breath and turned, ready to descend to my doom. Suddenly, out of the corner of my eye I saw something move. I wheeled about expecting to see Sarah or Nick. Instead, I saw The Thing!

Chapter Sixteen

THE PLAY! THE PLAY!

No doubt about it. It was the same creature I'd seen at the window the previous week. I wasn't likely to forget that big, round, hairy face.

The Thing had been crouched behind a pile of broken floorboards. That's why I'd missed it before. Now that it had raised its head I could see the monster for what it truly was.

A fat, gray and white pussycat.

He meowed and rubbed his cheek against a board.

A cat! All this time I'd thought The Thing was some horrible monster. I would have laughed if it hadn't been five minutes past noon.

"The play! The play! The play!" the crowd chanted.

I wasn't sure whether they were excited to

121

see our performance or simply anxious to double their money. It didn't really matter. At that moment all they wanted was me.

"So long, kitty," I said, before starting down the stairs. "Wish me luck."

"Meow," he replied. Which in cat language probably meant "Good luck, you're going to need it, you poor pathetic fool."

By the time I reached the bottom of the stairs, the crowd had begun pounding their hands on the floor in time to their chants.

"The play! The play! The play!"

I hooked my fingers under the straps of my overalls and looked around the room once more for Nick and Sarah. I couldn't believe they'd ditched me. Maybe they'd figured out I hadn't written anything. Still, I wished they'd had the decency to say good-bye.

"The play! The play! The play!"

I waved and stepped to the back of the room where a small spot had been cleared for the stage.

"The play! The play! The play!"

I raised my hand for quiet and the chanting stopped.

"Hey! Don't you want this?" shouted

someone sitting practically at my feet. I looked down and saw Teddy LaBone seated next to Will. He was holding up my black notebook in his gloved hand. He grinned and tossed me the book. "Here you go, Mr. W. Shakespeare."

I caught the notebook in mid-flight and gave him a look of disgust.

"Thief," I said.

"How could I be a thief?" he said. "I didn't steal anything. There was nothing in your book."

"Yeah, some great play," said Will sarcastically. He laughed.

"On with the show!" yelled a red-faced man in the back.

"In just a minute," I said, raising my hand.

"It's late already. I don't want to wait a minute!" replied the man, cupping a hand to his mouth.

The audience applauded. Apparently, they weren't interested in waiting a minute either.

I drew in a deep breath and fiddled nervously with the straps on my overalls. I didn't know what to do. The audience was waiting for a play that hadn't been written yet. And if they didn't get the play they were going to demand a ton of money that I didn't have.

I dawdled for what seemed like forever, waiting for inspiration to strike. I was a writer! Why couldn't I think of a story?

Meanwhile the crowd grew increasingly restless. "Go on. You can do it, dear," came my mother's voice from out of a distant corner. I looked her way. I would have done anything to have leapt into her arms at that point and been swept away to safety.

"Don't be afraid," shouted the man next to her. "Forge ahead, son. There's money at stake!"

I gasped. That was my father sitting next to my mom and Beth. He was the last person I expected to see. He thought entertainment was a waste of time, and he didn't think much of me either. I figured Mom probably dragged him there against his will.

"There's no play and there's no surprise ending," said Teddy, jumping to his feet. He turned and addressed the crowd. "Line up and let's get our money back."

"Double our money back!" shouted the crowd as one.

I couldn't wait another second for Sarah and

Nick. Right then and there I made two decisions. The first was never to speak to Nick and Sarah again. The second was to launch into the play.

"Quiet!" I yelled, raising my arms. "How can there be a play with all this noise?"

Teddy grumbled and sat back down. The crowd hushed and turned their eyes my way.

"Today's play is called 'The Thing Upstairs,' " I said. "It's all about a farmer, a monster, and a sergeant in the army."

Everyone laughed.

"It's very scary," I said. "Especially the part about the monster."

"What part is that?" someone shouted.

I didn't have the slightest idea, but I couldn't let anyone know that. If I let on that there was no play, even for a second, it was going to cost me a lot of money. "The scary part is at the end, of course," I said.

"Of course," I heard some people mutter.

"Once upon a time a horrible Thing lived upstairs," I said. "Some said The Thing was a monster. Some said The Thing was a zombie, half living, half dead."

The crowd hushed. Some of them leaned

forward. I had their attention. My words had moved them! I was a real writer!

Of course I wasn't likely to move them much further. I'd run out of words.

"Go on," I heard someone whisper. "What happens next?"

"A funeral," I muttered. "My own."

Chapter Seventeen
THE BIG SURPRISE

"Upstairs lives The Thing," I said, pointing at the ceiling. "Some say he's a monster. Some say he's a zombie, half living, half dead."

"We already heard that!" said Teddy.

Will kicked me in the foot. "You don't know anything. Give us our money."

Teddy and Will were right. I didn't have a play. My father was right. I'd been wasting my time pretending I was a writer.

Just then—*BAM!* Something banged against the ceiling.

"The Thing!" half a dozen people gasped.

Everyone looked up.

BAM! BAM! BAM!

"There it is!" I yelled, seizing the moment. "The Thing upstairs walks."

The audience shifted uneasily. Everyone's

eyes were on the ceiling.

BAM! BAM! BAM! It sounded as if the floor was being ripped apart.

I couldn't imagine what was making the noise, and I didn't care either. Whoever was banging around up there was helping me write the play.

"Sometimes The Thing likes to bang on the floor," I said. "He always does it right before he comes downstairs and picks out some people for lunch!"

Two people screamed. Others laughed nervously. I glanced down at Teddy and Will. Even they looked uncomfortable.

"We need to call out the army," I said, thinking of Sergeant Sarah. "Maybe they can stop him before the horror begins."

BAM! BAM! BAM! The noise kept growing louder. Before long the ceiling was shaking and bits of plaster were fluttering down like fat flakes of snow.

"Prepare to meet the awful beast!" I said, pointing at the stairs.

Just then, to my total surprise, the beast appeared.

At first the audience screamed. Then they

laughed as the awful Thing sat down on one of the steps and started licking himself. It was the gray and white cat.

"Big deal. It's just a kitty!" said Teddy.

"That's no surprise!" yelled the big man with the tangled beard.

"Give us our money back. I thought we were going to get The Thing!"

I winced. "That wasn't the best surprise you've ever seen?" I asked desperately.

"No!" three hundred people replied.

BAM! BAM! BAM!

Everyone looked at the cat, then up at the ceiling. Something else beside the cat had been making the noise!

Krr—ACK! A huge hunk of plaster broke loose and crashed to the floor right at my feet.

I leapt back and gazed up into the newly created hole.

BAM! BAM! The banging wouldn't stop.

Everyone edged forward and looked up.

KE-RASH! Another hunk of plaster broke loose and splattered onto the stage.

"Who's up there?" I yelled.

No one else in the room spoke. They must have thought I was still putting on the play.

129

When I didn't hear an answer I stepped directly under the hole and stared up.

"Yikes!" I screamed, momentarily frozen in place. Staring back at me from the space above the ceiling was the most awful creature I'd ever seen. Its face was nothing but a skull tightly covered by dried, brown skin. A few kinky strands of black hair stuck out of its head like old wire and the lips were pulled back, exposing yellow teeth in a silent scream.

I thought I might faint.

BLAM! Another blow to the floor made The Thing tumble halfway out of the ceiling. For a moment it hung upside down by its bony waist, swinging slowly, its long fingers—half bone, half flesh—dangling above me like fat worms.

"The Thing!" I yelled.

Some people in the crowd began gasping as if fighting for air. The Thing shifted again. There was a screeching, tearing sound as old bone scraped against wood.

Somehow I found the strength to step aside just as The Thing fell forward, then caught its heel on a piece of jagged plaster.

The crowd screamed so loud I thought my ears would explode. Some people started to cry.

Others tore at their hair. Way in the back I caught sight of my father, his eyes wide and his back pressed to the wall. Up front Teddy and Will were screaming like wounded crows.

Hanging by a single heel, The Thing swung forward, its hollow eyes searching the crowd for a victim while its yellow teeth awaited the first bite.

I opened my mouth to scream, but nothing came out.

Then The Thing fell. In slow motion it turned onto its stomach and bellyflopped onto the floor, crumpling slowly into a tangle of bone and rags.

KA-PING! One of the hands broke off and flew across the stage. Every eye in the place watched in horror as the withered, bony hand somersaulted through the air and landed in Teddy LaBone's lap.

"Yikes!" screamed Teddy, throwing his arms into the air. His hat went flying. His face turned white as paper. "Help! Help! Get it off!"

Having a skeleton hand land on top of you would be scary enough, but for Teddy the hand was only the beginning of the nightmare.

"Eeee-yarrrrgh!" he yelled. "Germs!"

Suddenly he was on his feet, wildly brushing at the spot where the hand had touched. "Skeletons and germs!" he shouted. "I'm going to die!"

For nearly a minute he danced in place, waving his arms and kicking out his legs as if somehow he could shake off the horror.

I looked down at the pathetic mess that had once been The Thing. Then I looked at Teddy. Despite all that had happened, I laughed.

The rest of the crowd wasn't nearly as amused. The room was in chaos. Everyone was shouting at once.

"The monster's loose!"

"Run for your lives!"

"Please! Please!" I said, raising my arms. "The Thing is dead. There's no need to panic!"

"Why not!" screamed a lady in the back. "Why shouldn't we panic? Great heavens, man, a monster just broke loose in here!"

I had to think fast. If I couldn't calm the crowd there would be a stampede for the exits. People would be hurt, maybe even killed.

"What's wrong with you folks?" I shouted, suddenly coming up with a perfect ending and the perfect solution to the danger. "It's only a play. The monster's make-believe!"

That stopped them cold. The crowd let out a sigh of relief. Some of them even looked embarrassed.

"Of course," I heard a man in the front say. "We were even warned there would be a surprise."

Those people who had started for the door giggled nervously and returned to their places. All of them but two.

The last I saw of Teddy LaBone, he was barreling out the door, still swatting at his body, with Will Pickens not far behind. I had a feeling they wouldn't be returning to collect double their money back.

"Is The Thing really dead?" asked Mr. Hammer from the back of the room.

"I think so," I said, unsure what The Thing really was.

Just as the crowd was starting to calm down, another round of banging started up from the second floor.

BAM! BAM! BAM!

"It's The Thing's friends!" someone shouted.

"They're coming for revenge!" screamed Mr. Hammer.

BLAM! Suddenly a leg came shooting out of the ceiling.

Once again the place exploded in screams. I screamed, too. But only for a second. That's how long it took me to recognize the army pants around the leg and the sneaker on its very human foot.

Chapter Eighteen
THE END

"Oh, my gosh!" I shouted, staring at the leg dangling above me.

"Is it another Thing?" asked Mr. Cole, the biology teacher from the high school.

"Is the play still going on?" asked Mrs. Reisman.

I didn't stick around to answer their questions. In a flash, I was up the stairs and onto the second floor.

"Sarah!" I called, frantically searching the jumbled mess of plaster and wood littering the floor. "Where are you?"

BAM! BAM! BAM!

Another series of kicks pinpointed her position, inside the closet at the back of the room.

Of course! The closet was directly above the stage.

I zigzagged through the broken wood and

135

twisted nails as if I was crossing a thorny patch in my bare feet. The closet door was jammed shut, but three good pulls popped it open.

"Sarah! Nick!" I exclaimed, discovering my friends bound and gagged on the closet floor. "What happened?"

Through their gags they muttered a reply, but I couldn't understand their muffled words.

They looked tired and dirty and scared. Sarah's leg was still stuck through the hole in the floor while Nick was balled up in a corner, his monkey suit covered with dust and dirt and his stuffed puppy at his side.

A moment later I'd removed their gags and ropes.

"I'm so glad you came," said Nick, hugging me so tight I thought my ribs would burst. He started to cry. "I thought we'd never get out."

"I was sure you guys had ditched me," I said. "What happened?"

"Will and Teddy kidnapped us while we were changing," said Nick. He wiped his eyes with the back of his hairy monkey arm. "They wanted to make sure the play was a flop."

Sarah stepped out of the closet and dusted off her uniform.

"Those two are going to pay," she said, narrowing her eyes. "You can't tie people up like this."

"They're in big trouble all right, even though they did save the play," I said.

"How did they save the play?" said Nick, wrinkling his face.

"Your banging knocked loose The Thing," I explained. "It was hidden in the ceiling right under the closet."

Nick gulped. "The Thing?" He looked around nervously. "Is it still loose in the museum?"

"Come on," I said, leading them toward the stairs. "I'll show you."

As we came downstairs the audience began to applaud.

"Bravo! Bravo! Bravo!" they yelled.

Way in the back, his arm upraised, leading the cheers, was my dad. I gave him a little wave and he smiled back. I don't think a smile ever made me feel quite so good. He liked the play!

Sarah and Nick looked around, confused.

"What's everybody clapping for?" asked Sarah.

"They're clapping for us," I said. "Together we just put on a play with the biggest surprise ending ever."

"Author! Author! Author!" the audience cheered.

I raised my arms. "Thanks," I shouted. "But the real star today was The Thing."

"Yuck!" said Sarah, suddenly noticing The Thing crumpled up on the floor. Mr. Cole, the science teacher, and Dr. Brown from the Natural History Museum were bent over the creature, examining its teeth.

"What is it?" asked Sarah, bending down.

"It's a caveman mummy," said Dr. Brown. "He's probably from out in the desert. After he died the dry air preserved him."

"Whoever found him must have sold him to the Oddity Museum," said Mr. Cole. "I remember seeing him here when I was a boy."

"I wonder what he was doing in the floor?" I asked.

"I'd only be guessing," said Dr. Brown. "But the museum owner must have hidden him there, thinking that someday he'd bring him out and reopen for business."

Sarah took another look at the mummy and shuddered. "With The Thing as the star maybe we *can* reopen," she said. "I bet we'd make a fortune."

"This mummy belongs to science now.

The End

There's a lot we can learn from studying this man," said Dr. Brown. He stood up and dusted off his hands. "Don't worry. The Natural History Museum will pay you well for him."

Sarah and I exchanged grins.

"Hey, where's Nick?" I said. "He should be sharing in this moment."

"He's sharing it with his new friend," said Sarah.

"New friend?" I said.

Sarah pointed over at the stairs. Nick was sitting on the bottom step, hugging the gray and white cat. "I don't think Nick cares about the money right now," she said. "He just got himself a pet, a real one." She rubbed the scar on her chin. "I can't tell you how good it makes me feel to see those two together."

Sarah didn't have to tell anyone anything. We all knew she thought it was her fault that Nick couldn't have a pet. Now everyone could clearly see how happy she was to have helped her brother find the perfect pet.

I watched Nick and the cat for a minute. They looked as if they'd been friends all their lives. For the two of them, the day couldn't have turned out any better.

"I'm so excited that you're going to fix this place up," said Mrs. Reisman, grabbing my elbow. "I can't wait till this theater is done."

"Theater?" I said.

"Well, of course," said Mrs. Reisman. "Crimson Beach needs a theater, especially one that puts on such terrific plays. I was on the edge of my seat the whole time. I've never seen anything so well written."

"My boy, the writer," said Dad, coming up from behind us. He put his arm around my shoulder and gave me a hug. "Looks like you made money and entertained everyone at the same time. That's quite an accomplishment."

"He's a real W. Shakespeare," said Mrs. Reisman.

"He's my son," said Dad, broadcasting the news to all who would listen.

I felt so proud I thought sunshine must have been bursting from my face. We were going to have our own theater, and I was going to write the plays. I closed my eyes and let the wonderful feeling wash over me. What a day this had been. I couldn't have imagined a better ending if I'd written it myself.